THE BEACHCOMBER

A CASE FILES SHORT STORY

RACHEL AMPHLETT

ONE

As soon as Julie saw the thick-set man walking along the desolate shoreline towards her, she knew there would be trouble.

She could sense it, like the incoming lightning storm that filled the air with burning ozone and malevolence, turning the sunset from reddish gold to angry indigo and staining the horizon.

Clenching her fists, inhaling the salt-heavy breeze that whipped her straggly brown hair around her neck and shoulders, she watched while he stumbled across the uneven pebbles and sand with his head down.

He was limping – a swaying motion that pitched him from side to side as if the storm had him in its clutches, unwilling to release him.

Where had he come from?

Scanning the entrance to the footpath she'd followed from the outer edges of the small coastal town, she realised his dogged progress would have taken him straight past it, not along it.

How long had he been walking towards her?

A lone concrete slipway served as the only other access to the sea here, but that was almost half a mile away, next to the council signs about beach safety and a black plastic waste bin with litter scattered on the pavement around it.

Beyond the slipway, terraced houses lined the narrow potholed road that weaved its way along the Cornish coastline.

The buildings jostled for position, whitewashed walls tainted with grey now that the storm was getting closer, their salt-covered windows peering at her from under slate tiles as she stared back at them.

A desolation clung to the place if it was lamenting the end of the summer season and the tourists that had lined its winding streets.

For now, it was shuttered, closed.

Was he staying in one of the half-empty guest houses, like her?

Had he checked in to the same one?

She hoped not.

This place, with its sheltered port and southerly aspect, was meant to be a refuge, designed as an emergency harbour during storms back in the days when ships relied on sails.

She was meant to be safe here, away from trouble, away from danger.

At least for a while.

Scowling, Julie moved closer to the lapping waves, her eyes downcast while she searched.

She didn't want company.

If she were honest, she wasn't sure exactly what she wanted, but the walk served to give her time to think, to process the jumbled memories and worries that permeated every waking hour when she wasn't scuffing over the sand and weaving between the tideline of dead fish, shells and seaweed.

She raised her gaze at a soft slurp of heavy footsteps and a surprised grunt, then staggered backwards.

She was so lost in thought that she had almost collided with him.

He flinched.

Most people did.

It was a natural reaction given the pitted patchwork flesh of her right cheek, the scars and new tissue angry and pink.

Sore.

Painful.

A natural reaction, except that a little more of her shrivelled away every time she experienced it.

'Burns?' he said, his brows knitting together. 'Nasty.'

She snorted at his directness, at the lack of concern in his voice.

There was a rough edge to it too – cigarettes probably, or perhaps years of shouting over loud machinery.

'Yes,' she said because he was right.

'There's a storm coming, by the look of it.'

On cue, thunder rumbled and shook the briny air – closer this time.

'What are you doing out here?'

He attempted casual but she could hear the worry nibbling away at the edges.

'Looking for stuff. Shells, glass. Things like that.'

'Beachcombing, you mean?'

'Yes.'

'Finding much?'

'Bits and pieces.'

She jiggled the plastic container in her hand, the movement rattling hag stones and shells against pieces of buffed sea glass.

Green and white.

No blue glass yet.

Pushing her hair away from her face, she inclined her head towards the darkening horizon. 'There'll be more in the morning. Usually is, after a storm. You never know what'll get washed up here – or so I'm told.'

Another flash of lightning tore across the sky.

'You're not from around here then?'

'No.'

He tilted his head and narrowed his eyes. 'Do I know you?'

She bit back a nervous laugh. 'I don't think so. Are you a local?'

'No.'

'Oh. What are you doing here?' She watched his expression change from feigned interest to hunted before he looked away, his gaze casting out to sea as if looking for a way to escape.

'I needed to get away for a while.'

Me too.

Julie squinted as the first splodges of rain smacked against her scars. 'I'd best go. It's going to get rough out here by the look of it.'

She managed a small smile, the skin around her mouth tight, new, while her heart rate quickened in fear.

'Look after yourself,' he called after her.

His next words were whipped away as the wind tore at the clouds on the horizon and churned the waves into a foaming mass full of foreboding.

TWO

Julie towelled her hair dry and applied the special cream to her face, wincing as the nerve endings jangled and protested.

Months.

Maybe years, the specialist said.

It depends.

Be patient.

Her hair had grown longer in the ten months since the fire, her fringe now hanging in dark curtains over her cheeks.

She twisted the lid on the grey-coloured plastic pot and placed it beside the bubble pack of painkillers before turning away from the washbasin, tweaking the pullcord for the bathroom light.

A streetlight farther along the lane illuminated the double room she rented, bathing the soft blankets that stretched across the iron-framed bed with a subtle glow.

All the fixtures and fittings were functional, clean, nothing more.

An ancient radiator hugged the wall under the window sill and a small television clung to a bracket above a pitted oak-effect dresser.

She turned away from it, ignoring the remote control that had been placed on top of the dresser.

She hadn't watched television after leaving the hospital in Exeter, too afraid to watch the news and unable to lose herself in serialised dramas that bore no resemblance to real life.

Her life.

She could hear the television through the thin plaster wall from the room next door though, a man's voice calling out at regular intervals. Odd words, a jumble of composers' names, cities, songs…

A quiz show, then.

Was he winning, or losing?

Rain lashed against the window, and she debated a moment whether to pull the curtains or watch the remnant storm as it passed overhead and rattled the roof tiles.

Then she saw him, standing at the top of the concrete ramp leading down to the beach, his body leaning into the encroaching wind.

He tipped his head to one side, and she spotted the minute spark and flare of a cigarette lighter.

The movement was subtle, but enough.

He hadn't recognised her, though.

Had he?

She should've asked his name.

She would've done, ten months ago.

He turned around to face the guest houses, his profile silhouetted while a final, almost defiant flash of lightning illuminated the coast road.

Julie reared backwards, sure he could see her watching him, but he didn't move, didn't react.

He simply stood, stock-still.

Was he watching her?

Or waiting for something – or someone?

She reached out and swished the curtains closed, then leaned across and flicked on the light above the bed, its beam billowing across the pillows and a dark pink velvet sash that covered the top half of the blankets.

She crossed to a wooden ottoman at the foot of the bed and opened the cheap suitcase that lay on top of it, extracting a well-worn T-shirt.

A favourite.

Something familiar, with the logo of a band embossed across the front that had split up over a decade ago.

A single wardrobe huddled beside the door, but she hadn't opened it since her arrival.

She had lied to the owner of the guesthouse

when she checked in. It was the first lie to pass her lips since she was sixteen years old.

This was her fifth day in the small Cornish harbour town but she hadn't unpacked yet.

She wasn't sure she would.

Not now.

Unpacking offered permanency to her visit, a commitment that she would stay.

The man on the beach had changed that with his rasping voice, uneven gait and enquiring eyes.

Julie undid the dressing gown, let it slip from her shoulders and pulled the T-shirt over her head, careful not to smear the ointment away.

She eyed the mobile phone on the small wooden table beside the bed that served as a nightstand.

Should she call?

The light went out, extinguished in a split second along with the sound of the television.

A muffled curse sounded through the wall, the other guest swearing at a now blank television.

A power cut.

Despite her breath pinching at her lungs, despite her spiked heart rate, Julie had to know.

Was it him?

She reached out her hands in the darkness, cursing when her toe caught the leg of the ancient bedframe and pain radiated through her foot. Limping, she made her way back to the window and ran her thumb down the curtains until she found the edge and peered around the soft fabric.

He wasn't there.

No, wait.

There – next to the plastic waste bin by the wall.

He was drenched now, his hair slicked back and his coat wringing wet while he hunched over and crossed the road.

Coming towards her.

Julie shrank back, trembling, unable to tear her eyes away.

He kept his head down though as if to ward off the deluge assaulting him while he leapt over the gutter and onto the pavement below her window.

She held her breath.

The man paused and reached into his jeans pocket as if he was looking for keys perhaps, and then he took off at a jog.

Her shoulders slumped a little as he disappeared around a kink in the lane.

She exhaled, then dropped her hand from the curtain and blinked as the power flickered back to life.

Her phone emitted a loud *ping*, the chime cutting through the rain hammering against the window as a single line of text appeared on the screen.

Are you OK?

No, she thought. I'm not.

I'm scared.

THREE

When Julie walked downstairs the next morning, a faint light shone through the stained glass insert at the top of the guest house's front door.

The storm had passed, but a vicious wind still beat against the uPVC surface and flapped the letterbox against its brass frame. The steady beat echoed off the narrow hallway walls while she crossed to a spacious dining room at the front of the house.

Patricia, the landlady, was standing at a table in the back corner and talking to a burly man in his late fifties, a copy of a local newspaper open beside him.

'Morning, Julie. Be with you in a minute. Just getting Gerald here sorted out so he can be on his way.'

The man's pale grey eyes shifted away from Julie's scars before a blush crept across his cheeks and then he looked away, rested his arm across the open page and cleared his throat.

'Thanks, Pat. No rush,' she murmured.

She shuffled across to the window, choosing the seat that faced the way the stranger had walked last night while giving her a clear view of the new guest.

A draught swirled between the ill-fitting sash and after arranging her cutlery the way she wanted it, she gathered her thick woollen cardigan around her waist and peered through the glass.

Where was he?

The net curtain sheltered her from view, pale sunlight reflecting off the ageing polyester, and she shuffled in her seat to stare out across the waves.

The wind sent clouds of sand twirling into the air, scudding across the pebbles and discarded piles of bladderwrack.

Closer to where she sat, at the top of the concrete ramp leading down to the beach, the black council rubbish bin was being shoved inch by inch along the pavement in a battle of wits against the wind.

Julie wondered if it might topple over or be tossed across the street or down the concrete slipway.

She craned her neck to see around the bend

in the lane but there was no sign of the man this morning.

Not yet.

'Right, black coffee as usual?'

Julie cried out, her sleeve snagging the knife handle.

It clanged against the side plate, and she reached out to straighten it before looking up at Pat, the woman's face puckered in concern.

'Sorry, love – didn't mean to make you jump.'

'I was miles away there.'

'Hungry?'

Recovering from her fright, Julie took the menu from her. 'Please could I have two sausages, a poached egg, tomato and toast on the side?'

'Any bacon today? You haven't tried that yet. We get it from a local—'

'No thanks.' She grimaced. 'I don't like the smell.'

'No problem. I'll take this through to the kitchen, and then I'll bring the coffee.'

'Thanks.'

A bergamot aroma drifted towards her while Gerald stirred his tea, the clink of the spoon reminiscent of halyards against masts in the harbour.

She turned back to the window as he flipped

to the next page of the newspaper and muttered under his breath.

Eyeing the undulating pebbles beyond the slipway, she wiggled her toes in her battered walking boots and watched while a woman leaned into the wind while she followed a motheaten terrier across the shingle.

The dog paused every few metres, raised its nose and sniffed the air before continuing, his wavering progress and that of his owner driven by whatever scent had caught his imagination.

'Here you go.'

Pat's voice called across from the doorway, and Julie looked over her shoulder as the woman advanced towards her with a steaming plate of food, a cafetiere, and a condiment basket balanced on a plastic tray.

Squeezing out tomato sauce on the side of the plate and adding a liberal sprinkling of black pepper, she heard the man on the other side of the room push his chair back with an exasperated sigh.

He said nothing to his host in farewell and stalked from the room, his brow furrowed.

Julie put down her knife and fork and pushed away the plate, her throat dry as she swallowed the remains of the tomato.

'You look troubled, love.' Pat moved efficiently around the abandoned table, collecting crockery and half-empty jam pots. She placed the newspaper on another table, out of her way while she cleaned.

'He didn't seem very friendly.'

The woman chuckled, placing the tray on the sideboard before returning with a cloth in her hand and wiping down the vinyl tablecloth.

'A busy man, Mr Porter. Visits once a month – I think he must have some sort of consulting job with the harbour. Boats and the like, anyway.'

Julie took a sip of coffee, willing her heart rate to settle. 'Has anyone been asking for me?'

'Not since that phone call three days ago.'

'Okay, thanks.' She turned to the window once more, feigning interest in a crisp packet that tumbled along the kerb beyond the front gate until Pat wandered from the room with the laden tray.

The moment the door swung shut, she scuttled across to the other table, picked up the newspaper and returned to her seat while she turned the pages.

When she'd first walked in, the man – Gerald – had slipped his elbow across the text down on the left-hand side but she had seen the bright coloured advertisement for a local business on the opposite page.

It was on page five.

Just a few lines and a map showing the

beaches between here and Plymouth, but enough.

Bad weather curtails Border Patrol efforts.

Exhaling, she ran her eyes down the text, noting an ongoing operation to thwart smuggling activities along the Cornish coastline.

Drugs, contraband cigarettes, alcohol – time had passed, but the old ways stubbornly refused to leave this part of the world.

Folding up the newspaper, Julie stared through the window, seeing nothing while she tried to grasp at a memory that kept sinking out of reach.

FOUR

There was a freshness to the air this morning and a bleakness to the washed-out sky when Julie crossed the road to the slipway.

Gulls stalked the pavement, keeping a wary eye on her while she unzipped the canvas satchel slung across her slight frame. They turned away once they realised the plastic container she pulled out was empty.

Her boots were still damp on the uppers from walking the shoreline yesterday, the toes sparkling with dried salt.

Both those and the padded jacket that came down to her knees had been purchased from a local charity shop in a hurry.

The boots pinched her toes and the cuffs didn't quite cover her wrists, but the clothes were serviceable.

Adequate for her needs.

She walked with her head down, searching.

Once a firm believer in turning over every stone to find what she sought, she now took her time, waiting for secrets to reveal themselves.

Some things, some people, didn't want to be found.

It would take time, she reminded herself, and she had plenty of that these days.

Her ankle rolled, her boot sliding over a seaweed-slicked rock, and she threw out her arms to steady herself, heart ratcheting up a notch in fear.

Taking a moment to steady herself, recalling the breathing exercises she'd been taught to calm her nerves, she looked over her shoulder.

A chill caressed her neck despite the thick woollen scarf she wore.

The man from yesterday was only a hundred metres or so behind her but she recognised the uneven gait, the way he kept his weight off his right knee.

A trail of smoke petered out above his bare head, cast away by the stiffening breeze.

Then he raised his hand in greeting.

She waited.

As he drew closer, Julie saw that he hadn't shaved.

A day's growth clung to his jawline and there were dark circles under his eyes that were more visible now than in the gloom of last night's storm.

He dashed the spent cigarette to the ground before shoving his hands in his pockets.

'You shouldn't do that,' she called. 'Those things take decades to decompose.'

'I'll bear that in mind.' He paused a few steps away from her and glared at the churning water. 'I thought the forecast said there'd be an improvement after the storm.'

'More on the way tonight apparently.' Julie inclined her head towards the slipway, now a good half a mile away. 'Did you have plans?'

He shrugged.

'Sort of. I was expecting someone but I think the storm delayed them.'

'I'd imagine the roads are flooded in places,' Julie said, switching the plastic container to her other hand and shoving her numb fingers into her pocket.

'Maybe that's it.' He forced a smile. 'Did it keep you awake, all that thunder?'

Julie swallowed.

'Only for a while,' she said eventually. 'I think all this fresh air tired me out. I couldn't keep my eyes open. What about you?'

'I couldn't sleep so I went for a walk.'

She turned her attention to the stones and shells once more, chancing a glance from under her overgrown fringe at the dark circles under his eyes and the growth on his jaw.

'Are you staying locally?' she asked casually.

'Close by, yes.'

'In one of the guest houses?'

'No.'

'Oh. Do you have friends here then?'

'None that I know of.' He turned away from her, cupped his hands around another cigarette, the flash of his lighter wavering in the wind before he exhaled the first nicotine-laden smoke skywards and flashed her a smile. 'Do you know anyone down this way?'

'No.'

'Then why did you come here?'

'I needed to get away.'

He chuckled, squinting as he peered out to sea. 'Yeah, that's what I said. You and me – I think we're similar. Both of us running until we couldn't go any further.'

We're nothing alike.

She scowled and turned away, her boots crunching over shingle and broken clam shells, eyes searching.

'What are you looking for today?'

He was following her, his footsteps only a few metres away, his gait as nonchalant as his words.

'Blue sea glass,' she said and kept going.

Another few paces forward, then—

'Why?'

'I'm not sure.' She paused, frowning. 'Actually, I think I do.'

He waited, amusement in his eyes through the pall of smoke before he kicked at a pebble. It scuffed across the sand, a wave covering it within seconds. 'Go on.'

'It's hard to find,' Julie said. 'So it's a challenge, you see. It gives me a purpose.'

'Do you need a purpose?'

'It helps.'

She said nothing more and turned away, leaving him to stare at the waves that lapped at his already sodden shoes.

FIVE

Julie was certain now that she'd seen him before.

A lifetime ago.

She perched on the edge of the bed, staring through the window while the stranger hobbled up the slipway from the beach.

She tried to imagine him without the beard, without the worry lines that scored his brow, but her memories pushed back and refused to cooperate.

He leaned against the wall when he reached the road, turning away with a wistful glance towards the broiling sea while he rubbed at his knee.

Evidently walking on the uneven beach aggravated the injury, so why did he do it?

He suddenly straightened, rolled his shoulders and crossed the road below her window, his awkward gait swinging him left and right.

Despite his apparent injury, he walked with purpose, resolve, and Julie wondered what had happened to spur him forward in such a rush before he turned towards the centre of the small town.

Groaning, she lay back and eyed the yellowing swirls of the plasterwork ceiling, an errant cobweb tangled amongst the light fitting swaying in the warmth rising from the radiator under the window sill.

Stay away, they told her to start with.

Then, after eight months, when are you coming back?

That's when she'd fled, packing one suitcase, ignoring the laptop gathering dust on the dining table, and only switching on her phone once a day.

At first, she'd been mortified at the number of missed calls and message notifications that peppered the screen.

Then she simply wondered when they would stop.

Give up hope of ever hearing from her again.

And now…

She ran a hand over her eyes and sat up, then blinked as a familiar figure came into view, his pace frantic.

Gerald hurried along the pavement towards the guest house, his heavy black wool coat open, flapping in the breeze. Face beetroot, his thin hair lifted in wisps as he stumbled up the short path to the front door.

Julie slid from the bed after it slammed shut, shoving her feet into canvas slip-ons and crept to the door.

Heavy footsteps took the stairs, laboured breaths echoing off the narrow landing as Gerald made his way past her room.

She opened the door a crack and heard him grunting under his breath while the sound of hangers slapping against the back of a wooden wardrobe carried to where she stood.

He emerged moments later.

Julie slipped the door back into its frame and held her breath as he walked past.

Stomping back down the stairs, he called out to Pat, then the small brass bell beside the complimentary tourist leaflets rang out.

'Pat? You there?' he called, his voice rasping between gasps.

Julie left her room and eased across the landing to the bannister.

Gerald was standing at the bottom of the stairs, a black canvas holdall at his feet.

He moved from one foot to the other and then spun around as Pat's voice carried from the direction of the kitchen.

'Everything okay?'

'I need to check out early, I'm afraid. There's been a sudden change of plans.'

'I'm sorry to hear that. Is there anything we can do to hel—'

'Just the bill. Thanks.'

'Give me a moment and I'll tot up your account. Will you be paying by card or—'

'Cash. Like last time.'

Julie frowned, sidling across the carpet and hoping the floorboards didn't creak.

Who the hell paid by cash these days?

And why the sudden need to leave?

Had he seen the stranger with the limp?

Did they know each other?

Pat returned, her cheery voice announcing what Gerald owed, then thanking him profusely at the generous tip he added to the cash he handed over.

'Not at all. I always appreciate your hospitality.'

'I do hope everything is all right though?'

'It is. Nothing to worry about.' His voice petered out as he disappeared from sight, and Julie realised he'd walked into the dining room. 'Have you seen my newspaper?'

'Newspaper?'

'Yes. The one I was reading this morning at breakfast.'

'I haven't I'm afraid. Our cleaning lady's just left for the day. If she put it in the recycling bin, it'll be long gone. The collection was an hour or so ago.'

'Dammit.'

'I'm so sorry. I can phone around and see if anyone has another copy?'

'No, no. There's no time.' He patted his pockets as he returned to the hallway, then pulled out a key fob. 'I need to go.'

With that, he picked up the canvas bag and hurried through the front door, leaving Pat muttering under her breath as she walked back to the kitchen.

Julie raced back to her room and went to the window.

She hadn't driven here, she'd taken the train and then two buses to reach her destination, but there was a small car park behind the terraced houses along the coast path, and she hoped Gerald had used it.

This road was the only way out of town.

She heard it first, then watched as a dark blue hatchback tore past the guesthouse, the driver hunched over the wheel as if trying to make it go faster along the narrow lane.

Automatically, she registered the licence plate, reciting it under her breath as she turned away and sought a pen and paper from her bag.

That done, she eyed the folded newspaper on the dresser, and then picked up her phone, dialling a number from memory.

No one answered.

Cursing, she left a message, her voice clipped

while she tried to condense her theory into cohesive instructions.

When she ended the call, she stared at the screen a moment longer.

Would they come?

Would they listen to her, after all this time?

She raised her gaze to the window, to the pebbles and sand, and to the churning waters beyond.

Hope.

There was always hope.

SIX

An agitated surf greeted Julie early the next morning.

Foam and kelp teased against the beach before being torn away once more, the seaweed a reluctant passenger on the retreating waves.

Pushing her unruly hair from her eyes and tugging down her woollen beanie over her ears to combat the wind, Julie's eyes swept the tideline, searching.

A pale pink coloured the sky now, an ominous sign of more unsettled hours ahead if the guesthouse's landlady was to be believed.

Julie didn't trust superstition – she had seen too much in her forty-two years – but she admitted to a sense of foreboding in the salty air as if this place held unfinished business for her.

She shivered and pulled her scarf up to her chin, careful not to snag the fluffy material against her scarred cheek.

Her eyes watered, sand catching on her lashes while she resumed searching the stony sand at her feet.

'Huh.'

Julie crouched, turned over a broken mollusc, then smiled at the bright blue glass that glinted under the weak morning sunlight.

'Found something interesting?'

She spun around, a sickness twisting her stomach as a familiar waft of nicotine blew in her face.

Coughing, she waved her hand in front of her face and blinked.

His head was cocked to one side while he watched her.

Julie held up the shard of blue glass, its edges softened by years tumbling within the sea's clutches.

'You managed to find some. Congratulations.'

'It's rare,' she said. 'These days, anyway.'

'A lucky find then.'

She smiled at his words, despite herself, and peered at the sea wall separating the beach from the coastal road and the tired guesthouses beyond before her eyes found his once again.

'It was, yes.'

'Why is it so rare?'

'They don't use it so much anymore. Everyone uses plastic these days.' A wave ran up the sand, lapping at her toes and she paused to watch the surf churning against the rocks farther along the beach. 'I wonder if it came from a shipwreck…'

'Plenty of wrecks here.' He smiled. 'Including us, right?'

She shivered, turning the blue remnant between her fingers, remembering the sound of glass splintering under intense heat and the burning sensation as splinters tore through her clothing, stabbing her skin.

'Are you all right?'

He reached out his hand, but she stepped away before he could touch her and dropped the sea glass into the plastic container where it landed with a clatter.

When she looked up again, she realised she was farther along the beach than before.

The small fishing village looked too far away, the walls of its horseshoe-shaped harbour a mere speck in the distance.

There was no one else in sight.

'I have to go,' she said. 'I made a mistake coming here on my own.'

'I didn't think to introduce myself properly yesterday.' He took a step closer and put the cigarette between his lips, then wrapped his fingers around her hand before she had a chance to recoil.

'I'm Joe.'

'Julie Nivens. What's your last name?'

'Whitely.' His smile faltered and he held onto her hand a little longer than might have been necessary, then frowned. 'Are you sure I don't know you?'

'We've never met, no.'

'Your name sounds familiar.'

She said nothing, her ears picking out the sound of shoes on gravel, and side-stepped around him, intent on looking at the thin strip of broken shells that washed in with the last wave.

He turned to watch as Julie bent her head to her task, then cleared his throat and tossed the cigarette stub to one side. 'So, how do you know what to look for, then?'

She couldn't prevent the smile that twitched at her lips, despite the salty air drying her skin, tightening it and sending pinpricks of pain around her jawline.

'I'm good at finding things, I suppose. Especially people.'

Enjoying the confused expression that flashed in his eyes before he took a step away from her, she jerked her chin over his shoulder to the four men who strode towards them, their gait faster now they had found their footing on the uneven surface.

Confusion turned to panic, then panic turned to tired resolution while he watched them.

The taller of the two signalled to the others to

fan out while he extracted a pair of handcuffs from his coat pocket, the steel gleaming under the pale light.

Whiteley turned back to Julie, his top lip curling.

'You…'

'Yes, me.'

Julie glared at him, a boldness returning that she hadn't felt in… too long.

'It was me who discovered where you'd been stockpiling your cocaine horde,' she said, her voice stronger now. 'We were searching the warehouse when you decided to firebomb it to try to hide the evidence. You killed a colleague of mine. A good friend.'

'He died while you managed to escape. A ceiling collapsed on top of him,' she added. Her fingertips fluttered to her right cheek. 'It was me who was trapped inside with no way out while the warehouse burned around me. And it was me who was rescued seconds before the roof caved in.'

A split second later, he was being cuffed by the detective, a man in his late forties who resembled a retired rugby player.

'It was Gerald, wasn't it? I told him he cocked up leaving that newspaper behind. That fucking reporter almost got my name right too,' Whiteley raged, spittle on his lips. 'I told him it was too risky to come here. I told him…'

'Joseph Markus Whiteley, you are under arrest…'

'How did you know I'd come here?' he managed. 'How did you know where to look for me?'

In reply, Julie lifted the plastic container and rattled it under his nose, the blue sea glass jostling for space amongst the tiny shells and stones.

'I told you,' she said. 'I'm good at finding things.'

Lowering her collection of finds before Whiteley was led away by two of the other plain-clothed police officers, Julie turned to the detective at her side.

'Looks like we found you just in time,' he said, his brow knitted together.

'You got my message then?'

'This morning – you were lucky. I wasn't meant to be on call until this afternoon.'

She exhaled, losing some of the tension in her shoulders. 'We got him, Lucas. We finally caught him. Here, of all bloody places.'

'Well, you did say you'd go to the ends of the earth to find him.' He grinned as she reached out to slap his arm.

His laughter faded, and then his eyes narrowed against the sand being whipped up by the wind.

He reached into his pocket and held out a slim black wallet to her.

'I think this belongs to you.'

When she opened it, tears traced the lines in her scarred cheek, blurring her vision.

A warrant card crinkled under the plastic protective cover, and she sniffed as her thumb traced the familiar creases in the leather.

'I take it that you're ready to come back to work, detective?' said Lucas.

Julie peered along the beach towards the battered guesthouses, the forlorn and shuttered windows staring sightlessly back at her, then turned back to her colleague.

'I am, yes.'

THE END

ABOUT THE AUTHOR

Rachel Amphlett is a USA Today bestselling author of crime fiction and spy thrillers, many of which have been translated worldwide.

Her novels are available in eBook, print, and audiobook formats from libraries and retailers as well as her website shop.

A keen traveller, Rachel has both Australian and British citizenship.

Find out more about Rachel's books at: www.rachelamphlett.com.

Blood on Snow

A suburban housewife is found dead in her garden. There is no weapon, no witnesses, and the only set of footprints belong to her cat.

Probationary detective Kay Hunter and her colleagues are convinced it's murder – but how can they find a killer when there are no clues?

ISBN eBook: 978-1-913498-70-2
ISBN paperback: 978-1-913498-71-9

The Reckoning

The newest arrival at a care home for the elderly carries an air of mystery that even an ex-WW2 Resistance fighter can't help trying to solve.

Then matters take a sinister turn…

ISBN eBook: 978-1-913498-70-2
ISBN paperback: 978-1-913498-71-9

www.ingramcontent.com/pod-product-compliance
Lightning Source LLC
Chambersburg PA
CBHW030846200726
48285CB00007B/2576